USBORNE FIRST READING
The Castle That Jack Built
Lesley Sims
Illustrated by
Mike Gordon

USBORNE FIRST READING
Danny the Drago
Russell Punter
Illustrated by
Peter Cottrill

USBORNE FIRST READING
The Boy
D0811475
Illustrated by
Mike and Carl Gordon

USBORNE FIRST READING
Chicken Licken
retold by
Russell Punter
Illustrated by Ann Kronheimer

USBORNE FIRST READING
Tom Thumb
Retold by Katie Daynes
Illustrated by
Wesley Robins

An Aesop's Fable
The Lion and the Mouse
Retold by Susanna Davidson
Illustrated by John Joven

An Aesop's Fable
The Town Mouse and the Country Mouse
Retold by Susanna Davidson
Illustrated by John Joven

USBORNE FIRST READING
The Magic Pear Tree
Retold by
Rosie Dickins
Illustrated by
Matt Ward

USBORNE FIRST READING
The Magic Porridge Pot
Based on the story by The Brothers Grimm
Illustrated by Mike and Carl Gordon

The Fox and the Crow

Retold by Susanna Davidson

Illustrated by John Joven

Reading consultant: Alison Kelly

Fox was greedy.

Fox loved food.

Fox was cunning.
Fox loved tricks.

But most of all,
Fox loved...

...CHEESE!

Yum!

So when Fox saw some cheese, Fox WANTED that cheese.

But Fox couldn't climb trees.

As for Crow...

Crow was *very* pleased.

“What a clever bird I am!” thought Crow.

Fox wasn't going to give up *that* easily.

There *must* be a way to get that cheese.

"You'll never do it,"
said Squirrel.

"Crow won't fall for your tricks," said Bear.

"Just you wait..." said Fox.

Yes! I've got one! And it might just work.

"Hello, Crow,"
called Fox.

"My! What a beautiful bird you are."

Crow looked down
at the crafty Fox.
I don't trust Fox.

"You have such glossy black feathers," Fox went on.

Crow puffed up
with pride.

"And you fly so well," said Fox.

"Oh I do," thought Crow. "I do!"

Bear and Squirrel looked at each other.

I don't know...
but I think Crow is
falling for it.

"I would love
to hear you
sing," said Fox.

"Such a beautiful bird must have a beautiful voice."

"Can I sing?"
wondered Crow.

"I always thought my
voice was a little...
well, croaky."

Crows can't sing!
Ha ha ha! What an idea!

I have glossy black feathers...
I'm a very clever cheese thief...

Maybe I'm also
a brilliant singer?

"I'm sure you sing much better than all the other birds," said Fox.

“What should I call you?” wondered Fox. “I know!”

"Oh! I'd like that!" thought Crow. "I'd like to be Ruler of the Birds."

So Crow began to sing...

CAWWWW!

Down fell the cheese!

Down...
Gone!

Fox snapped it up
in one gulp.

Delicious!

"Ha!" laughed Fox. "Your voice is terrible!"

"And a real ruler would never fall for that trick..."

Fox walked away,
looking *very* pleased.

"Oh dear," said Bear. "You should never have trusted Fox."

Fox only wanted your cheese.

"I know that now," snapped Crow.

Crow was *furious*.
"That Fox fooled me!"

"I'll NEVER be tricked by flattery again."

"I shall learn a lesson from this..." vowed Crow.

"Hello, Mouse. I've heard you are *very* clever..."

About the story

Aesop's Fables are from Ancient Greece. They always have a moral, or a lesson, at the end. The moral of this story is: "Don't be fooled by flattery."

Designed by Vickie Robinson
Series designer: Russell Punter
Series editor: Lesley Sims

First published in 2020 by Usborne Publishing Ltd., Usborne House, 83-85 Saffron Hill, London EC1N 8RT, England. usborne.com

USBORNE FIRST READING
Level Four

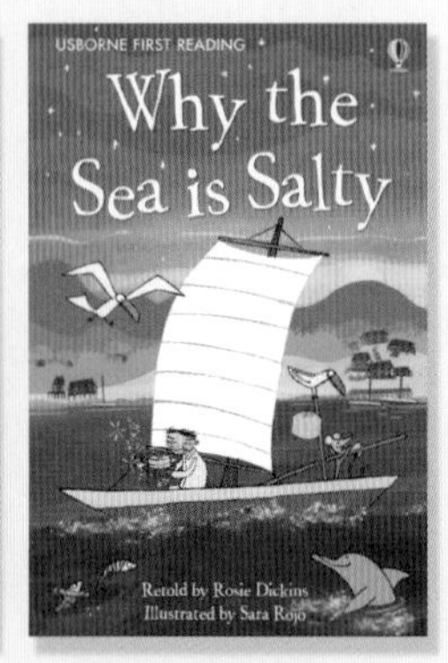